This book belongs to:

....

....

....

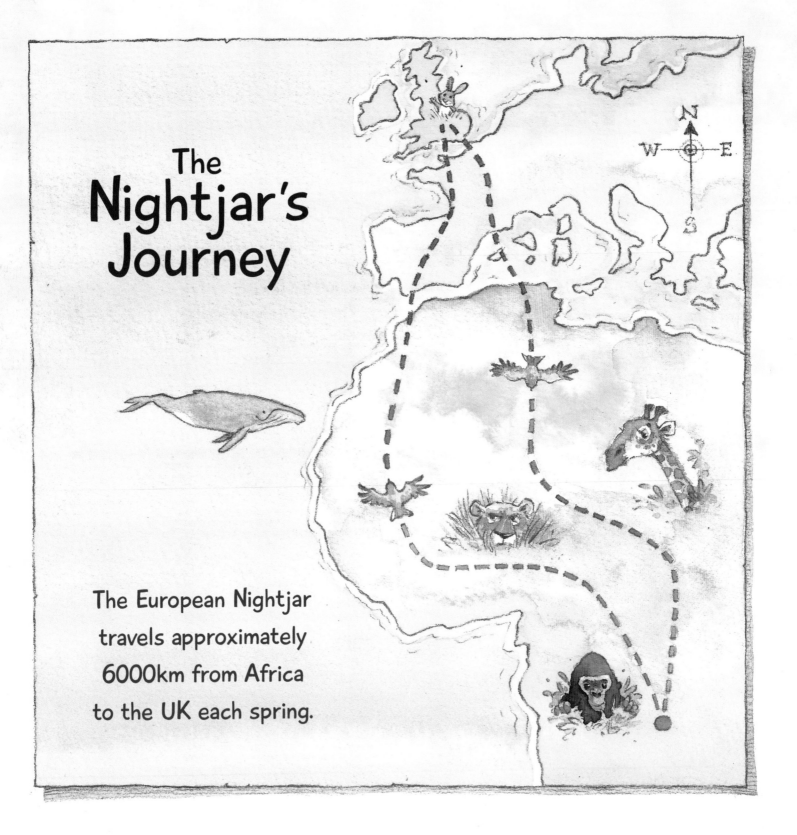

The Nightjar's Journey

The European Nightjar travels approximately 6000km from Africa to the UK each spring.

The Mysterious Bird in the Moonlight

by Steve Smallman

Late on a warm April evening,
As the last light seeped out of the sky,
The wind was as soft as a whisper,
And it moved through the reeds with a sigh.

In that mystical, magical twilight,
     In that pause between daytime and night,
A young rabbit lay still,
     calm, and peaceful until...

...an eerie sound gave him a **FRIGHT!**

CH

The sound seemed to be all around him:

A noise like a creaky old gate,

Or a rusty, mechanical monster.

It made Rabbit's whiskers vibrate!

¡¡¡¡¡RRRRRRRRRRRRR

'The Goatsucker's back!'
whispered Badger.

'I call him the Screech Hawk,'
said Deer.

'Gabble Ratchet!'
Toad spat.

'Razor Grinder!'
squeaked Bat,

And Rabbit's eyes widened with fear!

Poor Rabbit imagined a creature
    With terrible teeth and red eyes,
And he whispered,

'Deer,
does it eat...
          rabbits?'

'Oh, no!' Someone laughed...

…'Mostly flies!'

A mottled bird stood
there and chuckled,

'I eat beetles and dragonflies too —
And moths! (Some folk call me Moth Gobbler.)

But I *never* eat bunnies like you!'

'But Mr Bird,

what should I call you?

There are so many names I could use.'
    'That's true, I'm the Fern Owl, the Dor Hawk,
the Lich Fowl, the Nightjar!

I don't mind,
YOU CHOOSE!'

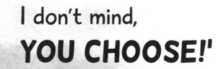

'And where did you come from?' asked Rabbit.
'From far, far away!' squeaked the Bat.

'Further away than
those trees?' Rabbit gasped.

The bird laughed,
'Much *further* than that!

'I've come from a land full of sunshine,
Where there's no snow, no ice, and no frost.
I fly thousands of miles just to get there and back:

I get tired but I *never* get lost.

Through dark stormy skies,
Through the wind and the rain,
I soar over mountains and trees.

I dip into rivers to
wash or to drink,

And then follow them
down to the seas.

I glide over sun sparkled oceans,

    Where the dolphins all leap up to greet me,

And whales wink an eye

    as they see me swoop by,

And the seals are *delighted* to meet me!

In steamy rainforests I sleep
through the day,
And nobody knows that
I'm there.

Then at night I take flight in the silver moonlight,
And pluck fireflies out of the air.'

'So why did you come back?'

YAWWWWNED Rabbit.

'To find a new wife,' the bird said,
 'And it's high time that I started looking,
And time you were tucked up in bed!'

The bird swooped up high and by moonlight,

He showed himself off at his best,

He flashed his white feathers,

His wings clapped together,

And someone was rather **IMPRESSED!**

The bird and his wife raised a family.

In a few weeks their chicks all took flight,

But he still found the time to tell stories
To a wide-eyed young rabbit each night.

Then one balmy evening in August,
'It's time,' the bird said, 'I must go.
Please, don't shed a tear! I'll come back next year,
But there's something I'm dying to know:

I said you could choose what to call me,
What did you decide in the end?
Am I the Nightjar? The Lich Fowl? The Fern Owl?'

The Rabbit said,
'No, just my friend.'